FOR FRANKIE, MILO, AND MARNI

-K.D.

FOR LAURIE LOWE
(AND FOR THE OCTICORN IN ALL OF US)

-J.L.

Balzer + Bray is an imprint of HarperCollins Publishers.

Hello, My Name Is Octicorn

Since this is just legal copy that no one will read anyway, we are hiding another dedication here: For Dani Guralnick, Janet Champ, Michael Folino—and for everyone who ever felt different. —Justin and Kevin

Library of Congress Control Number: 2015951002
ISBN 978-0-06-238793-6

16 17 18 19 20 SCP 10 9 8 7 6 5 4 3 2 1
❖
Previously published in somewhat different form by Octicorn Studios in 2013.
First HarperCollins Children's Books Edition

HELLO, MY NAME IS

OCTICORN

CREATED BY

KEVIN DILLER & JUSTIN LOWE

ADDITIONAL ILLUSTRATIONS BY

BINNY TALIB

BALZER + BRAY

An Imprint of HarperCollins*Publishers*

HI, EVERYONE. I'M OCTI.

WHAT?

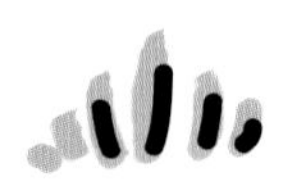

HAVEN'T YOU EVER SEEN AN OCTICORN BEFORE?

WE'RE HALF OCTOPUS, HALF UNICORN.
SO OKAY, MAYBE WE ARE KIND OF RARE.

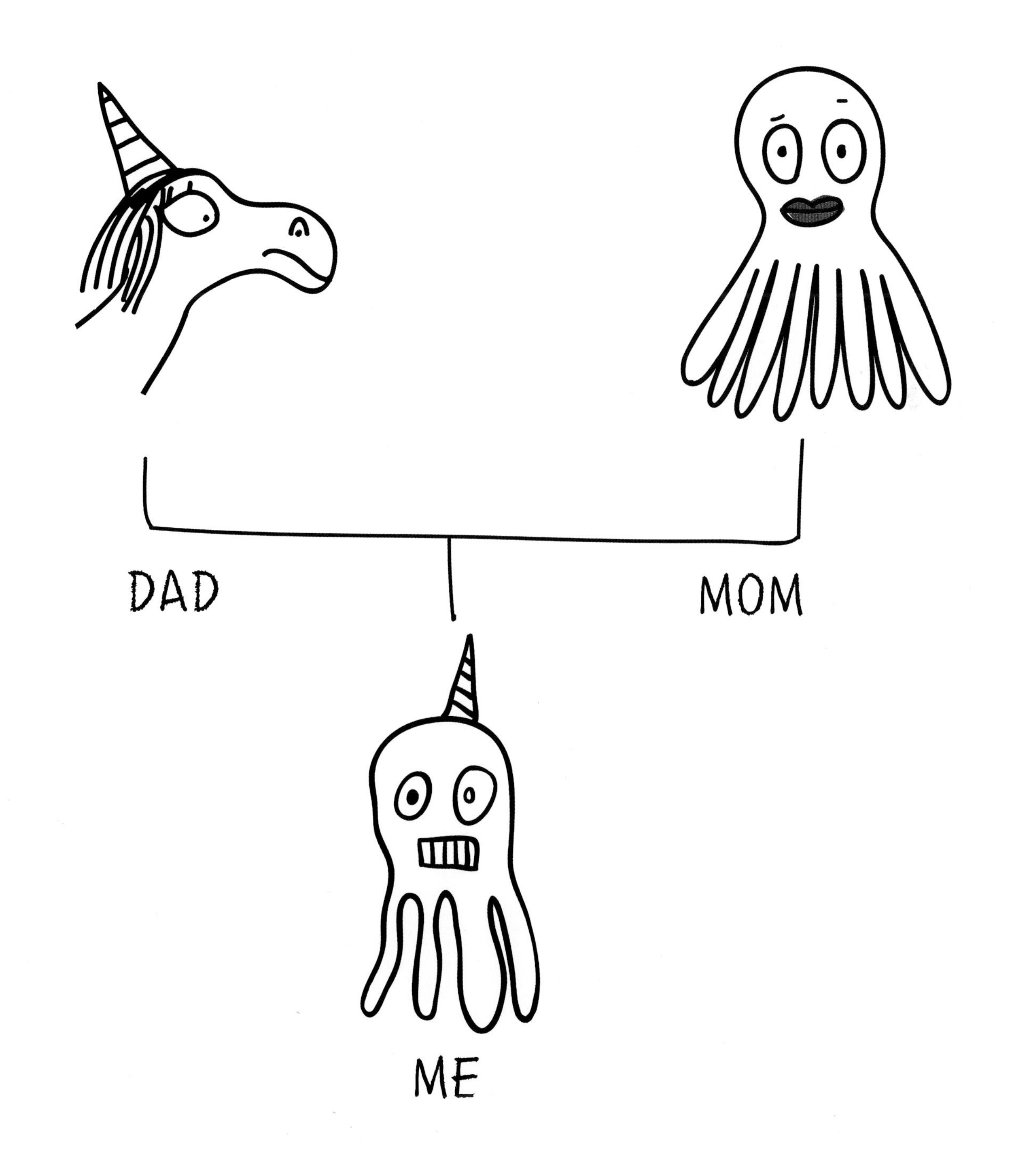
DAD
MOM
ME

NOT LIKE THE UNICORN SIDE OF MY FAMILY,
WHICH YOU SEE EVERYWHERE.

PERSONALLY, I DON'T GET WHY PEOPLE LIKE UNICORNS SO MUCH. I MEAN, EVEN JUST THE NAME. UNICORN. SHOULDN'T IT BE UNI-HORN? WHERE DOES THE CORN COME IN?

PLUS, IF YOU ASK ME, UNICORNS ARE
A LITTLE FULL OF THEMSELVES.

BUT BACK TO ME.

PEOPLE ALWAYS ASK HOW I CAME TO BE AN OCTICORN AND HOW MY PARENTS MET. I THINK IT WAS A COSTUME PARTY.

UNICORN
Seeks Octopus

for fun, friendship, and possible
strange-looking offspring.

OR MAYBE A PERSONAL AD.

AS FAR AS I KNOW, I'M THE ONLY OCTICORN THERE IS. WHICH SOMETIMES MAKES IT HARD TO FIT IN . . .

ON LAND . . .

OR AT SEA . . .

AND WHEN YOU DON'T FIT IN, YOU DON'T GET INVITED TO A LOT OF PARTIES.

FRANKIE
MILO
SID
ANABELLE
HUDSON
GUS
ROSE
LEO
ALICE
ELIAS
OCTI
LOLA
INEZ

WHICH IS TOO BAD, BECAUSE OCTICORNS ARE LOTS OF FUN AT PARTIES. FOR ONE THING, WE CAN JUGGLE LIKE NOBODY'S BUSINESS.

FOR ANOTHER, WE'RE QUITE GOOD AT CERTAIN GAMES, LIKE RING TOSS.

POP!

AND IF IT HAPPENS TO BE A POOL PARTY, OCTICORNS ARE GREAT AT WATER SPORTS. (EVEN IF THERE IS THE OCCASIONAL BEACH-BALL INCIDENT.)

OR IF YOU'RE NOT HAVING A POOL PARTY, HERE'S WHY YOU SHOULD STILL THINK ABOUT HAVING AN OCTICORN FOR A FRIEND:

OCTICORNS ARE GOOD AT LOTS OF SPORTS.

WE'RE ALSO TERRIFIC DANCERS.

OCTICORNS ARE EXCELLENT SWIMMERS BUT . . .
WHAT I REALLY WANT IS A JET SKI.

OCTICORNS LOVE S'MORES.

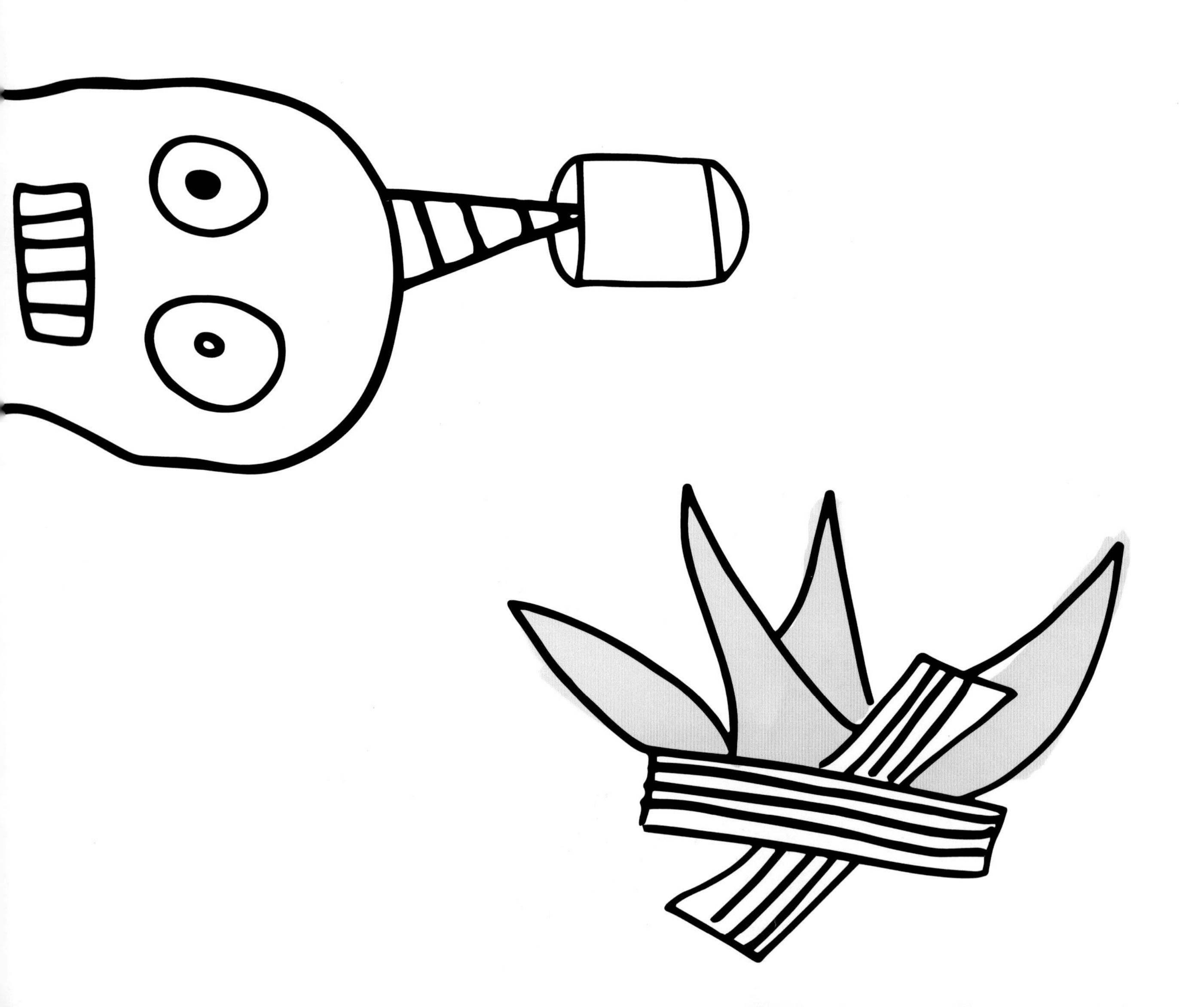

AND RECESS TOO, EVEN IF
IT CAN GET A BIT TRICKY SOMETIMES.

OUR FAVORITE COLOR IS BLUE, LIKE SKY BLUE
OR SEA BLUE OR COTTON-CANDY BLUE.

SOMETIMES OCTICORNS *FEEL* BLUE TOO. . . .

BUT OCTICORNS ARE EXTRA GOOD AT HUGGING,
WHICH USUALLY MAKES EVERYTHING BETTER.

OCTICORN HUG, ANYONE?

AND IF YOU'RE WONDERING WHAT TO SERVE AN OCTICORN FOR LUNCH, WE LOVE PLANKTON, FRESH CLOVER . . .

. . . AND ALSO CUPCAKES.

BECAUSE WHO DOESN'T LIKE CUPCAKES?

I KNOW I LOOK DIFFERENT THAN EVERYONE ELSE,

BUT THAT'S OKAY.

BECAUSE IN THE END, WE ALL WANT THE SAME THINGS: CUPCAKES, FRIENDS, AND A JET SKI.

SO, UM . . .

WILL YOU BE
MY FRIEND?
YES
NO

AWAITING YOUR REPLY . . .

LOVE,

OCTI